Well, it's not quite true to say WHITE.
Tiger Harry was the same colour that the other tigers were under their stripes.
Harry just lacked the stripes.
All his life, he had felt so SILLY.

Mr. Toffy, the ringmaster, tried all kinds of ways to cheer Harry up.

Once he gave him a pair of striped pyjamas to wear.

Harry tried them on, but took them off again immediately, saying he felt a right fool . . . the only tiger in the world in pyjamas!

Mr. Toffy had to admit that striped pyjamas didn't make a white tiger look like a real tiger anyway.

Bop the baggy clown had quite a good idea to solve the problem. (Bop's real name was Norman Peers, but Mr. Toffy made him change it, as Norman Peers wasn't the right sort of name for a clown.)

Bop's idea was to paint stripes onto Harry. The trouble was that Bop didn't have enough tiger-stripe coloured paint, and had to finish off in blue.

This made the other tigers laugh, and Harry didn't like it either because, apart from looking funny, he kept sticking to chairs.

Big Ethel, the hippo, had the most unpopular idea of all. She said:
'Why not paint all the other tigers white, then Harry will look just the same!'
The other tigers threw their dinner at Big Ethel.
Then something happened that was the last straw!

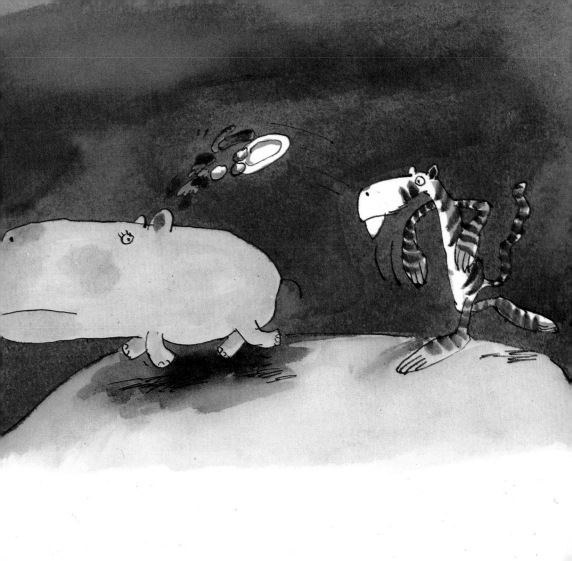

Tiger Harry was taking his late stroll, when a Police car screeched to a halt beside him.

Two large policeman bundled Harry into the car.

'One of Ted's sheep loose again' said one of them, turning the car in the direction of Ted's farm. 'Soon have him back again.'

'I'm NOT a SHEEP' screeched Harry, 'I'm a TIGER!'

'Tigers aren't white' observed one of the policemen.

'This one is!' shouted Harry. 'Look at my tail, look at my claws.'

Harry waved his claws and tail.

'Growl like a Tiger then' challenged the other policeman.

'GRRRRRRRR' growled Harry to oblige.

The policemen looked at each other. 'I think we've got a tiger here,' gasped one.

'I—I—I think you're right' answered the other.

The first policeman looked at Harry and put on his most official voice: 'Off you go this time,' he said, 'but don't go about pretending to be a sheep, or you'll be in trouble'.

'Cheek!' thought Harry, as he slunk home through the night.

The next day Tiger Harry was so upset that he wouldn't come out of his cage.

THE HUMILIATION, a tiger being mistaken for a sheep! He wouldn't eat his egg in the morning, and he wouldn't talk to anyone.

'Come on Old Lad,' coaxed Mr. Toffy later, 'all the other tigers are practising jumping through hoops. Come and join 'em'.

'I wish to be alone,' murmured Harry, looking the other way.

Harry couldn't sleep.

He prowled around his cage in the moonlight.

'Oh, I may as well go for a walk' he snarled, opening the door of his cage.

He walked all night, a long, long way. Tiger Harry liked the dark, because no one could see how funny he looked.

At last the sun began to peep over the roofs of the town. Harry was so tired that he crept over to a big fence and flopped down for forty winks.

Harry had more than FORTY winks, more like FORTY MILLION, for when he awoke he was very hungry and the long shadows of evening were growing.

'Cripes!' he gasped, 'I've been asleep all day.'

It was only when he jumped up that he saw the STRIPES all over him.

He stared at his striped paws, he gaped at his striped tail, he squinted at his striped back.

REAL TIGER STRIPES!

'OH BOY, OH, BOY' shouted Harry, bounding off in the direction of the circus.

As soon as he got back, Harry ran up to Mr. Toffy.
'I'm all stripey!' he squealed happily. He went on to tell
Mr. Toffy all about finding the new stripes.
'How did it happen Mr. Toffy?' he finished.
'Silly old thing' laughed Mr. Toffy, 'it was the sun! You
were asleep behind a fence, and the sun shone through,
and sunburned you in stripes!'
'Will the stripes last?' asked Harry anxiously.
'Sunburn always lasts on tigers!' smiled Mr. Toffy,
'ALWAYS.'